THE FALLEN

THE FALLEN

As Above, So Below
A Thriller from the World of Consciousness

A Novella

JAMES A. CUSUMANO

The Fallen is dedicated to two special friends—Deepak Chopra, who taught me the power of mindfulness and spirit, and Rinaldo Brutoco, who through his creative efforts at the World Business Academy, has demonstrated how technology and business linked to mindfulness and spirit can elevate global social consciousness. Working together, these two giants continue to design a path to save humanity from itself and create a sustainable future.

Books
by
James A. Cusumano

Freedom from Mid-East Oil
(Coauthors: Jerry B. Brown and Rinaldo S. Brutoco)

Cosmic Consciousness
A Journey to Well-being, Happiness and Success

Balance: The Business-Life Connection

Life Is Beautiful: 12 Universal Rules

ACKNOWLEDGEMENTS

Early drafts of this novella were read and critiqued by my wife Inez, my daughter Polly Cole and my sister Camille Cusumano, an accomplished author in her own right. I am deeply grateful to each of them for their valuable and constructive commentary.

TABLE OF CONTENTS

THIS SERIES

The Fallen is the first in a series of forthcoming novellas that weave together fictional stories from the thriller genre with concepts from metaphysics, mindfulness, science and technology. Each novella is about one-third the size of an average 300-page novel. They address controversial and hopefully, stimulating subjects in a straight- forward, non-technical manner and can be read in less than two hours at average reading speed—a kind of "small book for short flights!"

This first novella, *The Fallen* is a fictional thriller that taps into the power of *Cosmic Consciousness* as well as mindfulness and Eastern Wisdom concepts as a means to explore and explain tragic events that befall the protagonist, Michael Pierce.

Future books treat subjects such as hypnotically-induced remote viewing to distant celestial worlds, the unique power of an optimal ratio of feminine-to-masculine energies, instantaneous induction of higher consciousness in millions of people and a new beginning for a new world order, among others.

I hope to stimulate your thinking about new possibilities above and beyond so- called *well-proven, logical* concepts.

Enjoy your read!

James A. Cusumano
Prague
August, 2016
www.JamesCusumano.Com

DISCLAIMER

This book is a work of fiction and should be read as such. Many of the names, characters, places and incidents used in this book are products of the author's imagination. Historical, religious or mythological characters and events and places are used fictitiously. Any resemblance to any actual persons, living or dead, past events or historical locations, is entirely coincidental. While some notable persons, places and concepts are not fictitious, attempts have been made to blend references to them seamlessly with those of fictitious persons, places and concepts for the purpose of reader entertainment. The prime objective of the author in taking this approach is to stimulate and stretch the thinking of the reader concerning the real and potential impact of consciousness and mindfulness in our lives.

PREFACE

"Writing fiction is the act of weaving a series of lies to arrive at a greater truth." —**Khaled Hosseini**

Most of us go through an entire lifetime believing there's a logical explanation for everything that happens. Generally, that's a reasonable assumption. But, every now and then, we encounter experiences that defy our very notion of logic. Sometimes it can be deeply disturbing; and on occasion, even deadly. However, in the right context, such an experience can have an enlightening outcome. Such was the case for Michael Pierce, an intelligent, well-grounded and successful entrepreneur. For just a few seconds, he inadvertently stepped into an alternate dimension of space and time, into the "Twilight Zone"—and it changed his life forever.

CHAPTER 1
RENAISSANCE MAN

"While I thought that I was learning how to live, I have been learning how to die."—Leonardo da Vinci

Michael Pierce closed his eyes momentarily, and slowly sipped a vintage *Chassagne-Montrachet* Burgundy from an antique Baccarat wine glass. He only infrequently imbibed in alcoholic beverages, especially during the day, but this was a very special occasion. And when he did partake, it had to be an outstanding vintage. *If you are going to tranquilize your senses, it should be with the best quality drug you can choose.*

Michael was lost in a deep hypnotic reverie, a kind of open-eyed mediation, relishing his first day in a newly acquired penthouse apartment on the 55th floor of the *Tour De Versailles* Luxury Condominiums on Manhattan's Upper East Side. He had no idea of the terror that was about to enter his perfect life.

At 30, Michael was strappingly handsome and physically well-maintained by early morning visits to the gym as well as a strict healthy diet. Over the years, he had developed a strong commitment to life balance and purpose. He discovered early on that this was the true path to long-term fulfillment.

As a teenager, Michael began studies with Bankei Yōtaku, a Buddhist master, earning a black belt in aikido and a lifelong commitment to Eastern philosophy. He continued to meet occasionally with Bankei to sharpen and enhance his growth in

Buddhist wisdom. This training provided him with deep insight into the value and power of the martial arts, daily meditation and mindfulness. An hour of deep meditation punctuated his daily workout. Michael had what most would consider a high level of consciousness. However, he was not a stoic; he was a fun guy to be around. Friends and family loved him.

A true Renaissance man with many interests beyond his business predilections, Michael liked to cook healthy, tasty dishes for him and his friends, and when he did imbibe, he enjoyed the highest quality wines, generally one glass with meals, but never more than two. His mindfulness training would not tolerate more. He travelled to exotic places such as Tibet, the Arctic, Antarctica and Mongolia, and had a long-time interest and practice in high-altitude mountain climbing.

After reading Jon Krakauer's bestselling book, *Into Thin Air*, summiting the highest peak in each of the seven continents became one of Michael's passions. With some training and limited difficulty, his mental and physical acuities enabled Michael to conquer six of these giants—Aconcagua in South America, Kilimanjaro in Africa, Elbrus in Europe, Denali in North America, Vinson Massif in Antarctica and Kosciuszko in Australia. But after the death of world-famous climber Scott Fisher and several of his team on Mt. Everest during a flash blizzard on May 11, 1996, Michael decided to forgo his final conquest. His mountaineering friends never questioned his decision. Most professional climbers think of Denali as a more challenging climb than Everest because of its extremely cold temperatures and frequent rapidly changing weather. More than 100 climbers have lost their lives on that mountain.

Beyond his many outside interests, Michael was clever, resourceful and charismatic enough to have founded and led the growth of two public companies within the last several years. Cashing out with more than $250 million in personal assets made just about anything possible for him.

After college, he moved to Palo Alto, California to put his efforts into social entrepreneurship. He was recruited by one of the more successful Silicon Valley venture capital firms to lead a promising IT start-up as its CEO. The company focused on unique and proven technologies that made life easier for the disabled. After two years and an IPO on the New York Stock Exchange, he was a multi-millionaire with lots of opportunities. He succeeded in a repeat performance leading a company that developed and marketed state-of-the-art prosthetics—Silicon Valley's model for a serial entrepreneur. The rest is history.

Michael married at 24, but within two years suffered a personal tragedy, the loss of the love-of-his-life to brain cancer. Through his personal dedication to *Life Purpose* and *Consciousness*, he overcame his deep sense of loss. Having never remarried, meant that his fortune was all his, although he had plans to give most of it away, well before approaching old age.

Michael also had an unfortunate beginning. He was an only child whose mother died during childbirth. He never really knew his father, Patrick, a brilliant, tough-minded businessman who, unbeknownst to Michael, ventured all too frequently into the netherworld of the New York crime scene. At Michael's third birthday party, held at the home of his maternal grandmother Sophia, his father received a phone call and left for a short business meeting. He never returned—ever. But the curves that destiny threw at Michael made him stronger and were part of the reason he was so successful, as measured by just about any social metric.

Michael was raised by Sophia until he entered New York University to study economics and then moved on to Harvard for an MBA after a one-year stint at J.P. Morgan as an associate investment banker. On completing his MBA, he was heavily recruited by J.P. Morgan executives who offered him a huge starting salary and an enviable bonus incentive. However, a focus simply on financial success didn't appeal to Michael's social-entrepreneurial spirit, which is why he instead moved to

Silicon Valley. He yearned to be in the throes of creating and commercializing technology to make this a better world. Michael was more about *Life Purpose* than money; but the money always seemed to appear as a result of his successes. He often counseled his management team, "Don't follow the money! Do what you love, love what you do, and the money will follow!"

All of this said, he was about to encounter a world he was not prepared for. It would test his values, his consciousness and the very essence of his being.

CHAPTER 2
THE FALL

"There is nothing more deceptive than an obvious fact."—
Arthur Conan Doyle,

Michael sat fixated in a semi-trance, enjoying the subtle fragrance and taste of his vintage Burgundy. In his relaxed reverie, he thought, *this wine is a perfect example of Yin-Yang—opposite, complementary, yet interconnected forces. The Buddhists would say they are interdependent in our five-sense natural world, and give rise to each other as they spiritually interrelate. On one hand, a certain amount of wine can dissolve your fears and judgment; on another, it can lower your values to those of a more primal state. Amazing!*

As he contemplated whether or not to pour a second glass, his view through the huge sliding glass door to the terrace was abruptly interrupted by a horrific scene. In what was a mere couple of seconds, but to Michael's keen observation skills seemed longer and in slow motion, a well-dressed man in a pin-striped double-breasted suit fell from the high rise building directly across on Park Avenue. Distraught, terrified and panic stricken—feelings Michael had never experienced before—he rapidly slid open the terrace door, ran to the rail and looked down in horror to the street below.

But ... there was nothing there! Just people milling around on the sidewalk and cars and taxis honking their way to their destinations. "Good grief, am I dreaming?" After a second and then a third look to the street below, Michael slowly returned to his *Chassagne-Montrachet,* stood silently for a long moment, and then refilled his glass. He stood there in quiet mental disarray, rubbing the glass, then put it down without touching the wine and moved to his bedroom, falling on the bed, staring blankly at the ceiling.

Nothing like this had ever even remotely happened to Michael. He was a logical, well grounded individual. He didn't do drugs and had no emotional or psychological imbalances. He lay there for awhile in deep thoughtless contemplation, a kind of open- eyed meditation and a byproduct of his frequent practice of mindfulness. Not sure what to do, he decided to go for a run in Central Park to work through what had just happened. In addition to his daily morning meditation, Michael found running a kinetic form of mindfulness. The run was invigorating, but unfortunately, it was of no help in explaining what had just happened across from his condo.

Michael desperately wanted to see Sophia and Bankei. But Sophia was in Boston visiting a sick friend, and wouldn't be home until tomorrow. And Bankei was on his way back from India and would not arrive at his dojo and apartment for another two days.

He decided to try to clear, or at least occupy, his mind by arranging a date with Sheila, one of several stunningly beautiful women he was currently dating. With his looks, wealth, and smarts, he was one of the most sought-after bachelors on the chic Manhattan scene. Most of these cosmopolitan goddesses knew Michael had no designs on marriage, but each thought they might just change his mind; or at least have fun trying.

They went to Le Bernardin on West 51st Street, Michael's favorite spot for seafood in Manhattan. It usually required four to five weeks time to get a reservation, but Michael knew that Jonathan, the maître d', always kept two free tables for last minute calls from VIP customers; and those two tables were taken nearly every evening. Luck prevailed; there was one table left. Brad Pitt and Angelina Jolie had taken the other.

Michael's exceptional frame-of-mind encouraged him to quaff more alcohol than he had in a bundle of years. They finished a bottle of Dom Perignon—Sheila drank most of it—and a bottle of 1987 Chateau Petrus. Michael drank more than his two-glass limit to accompany his favorite dish, Bacalao "Serenata." It wasn't long before Sheila convinced him to head back to his apartment, where they broke in his brand new custom- designed Saffron bed. After an hour of Kama Sutra, they fell into an oblivion of deep slumber.

Several hours later, Michael squirmed as he entered a violent nightmare. The horrific vision appeared again—a man falling, falling, falling—continuously falling and screaming at an incredible volume from the building across the way on Park Avenue. But, who was it? When did it happen, if ever? And, why? Even in his nightmare, these questions haunted Michael's soul. And things would get worse before they got better.

Chapter 3
Take Two

"It's déjà vu all over again." —**Yogi Berra**

Michael awoke with a start, trying to gather his thoughts through the fog of a hefty hangover, something he had not experienced since his freshman year at NYU. He never overdid his alcohol intake, but yesterday afternoon's apparent "virtual" tragedy was so *real* and much more than just a disquieting experience. He squinted at the clock on his nightstand—3:00 a.m. *Damn, too much wine—and too much Sheila. My god, what in the world was I thinking—or not thinking?*

Sheila was sound asleep, and looked like she might never wake up. He slipped on his robe and ambled to the kitchen and poured some crushed ice and water from the fridge. Shuffling slowly to the living room, he alternately sipped on the ice water and then put the glass to his temple trying to clear his mind and ease the throbbing pain in his head.

Staring out the window, Michael had momentarily forgotten about his nightmare and the frightening event of yesterday afternoon. He aimlessly began to admire the details of the December holiday decorations on the building across the way. It was lit up like a giant Christmas tree and the staccato dance of flashing colored lights reminded him of his early childhood.

Every Christmas, Sophia would bring Michael to see the celebratory lighting of the huge Christmas tree at the ice-skating rink in Rockefeller Plaza and then to the annual holiday show at Radio City Music Hall, featuring the beautiful and sensual high-stepping Rockettes. He loved their colorful costumes, their statuesque beauty, and the precision with which all thirty-six of the dancers kicked and moved like a drill team of Greek goddesses. He also was transfixed by the talented organ player, who magically rose up through a trapdoor on the stage floor and warmed up the crowd before the show began. In the dreaminess of the moment, he could still feel the massaging vibrations of the dramatic organ music running up and down his spine as he replayed in his mind's eye, Sammy Cahn's, *Let It Snow! Let It Snow! Let It Snow!* It was a very special time for both Michael and Sophia.

Seamlessly merging his childhood nostalgia with the hypnotic Christmas decor on the building across the way, Michael felt himself beginning to transition to a meditative state he had skillfully taught himself over the years. It was a method he had learned from modern-day spiritualist, Neville Goddard. The technique was best practiced in the evenings, just before going to sleep. It was an altered state-of-consciousness that allowed him to keep his eyes open, if he chose to do so. Its primary purpose was to quiet the conscious babbling "monkey" mind and have complete access to the subconscious mind, the force that's in charge of nearly all of our actions.

Michael had learned long ago from Bankei that *the subconscious mind is what you are and the conscious mind is what you know.* It was therefore most important that the "tapes" in your subconscious were directly in accord with you true values. When practiced correctly, it was possible to edit and reprogram the subconscious, adding instructions you desired and erasing those that were undesirable. For Michael this was a powerful tool to manifest just about anything he desired into his life.

As he was just about to complete transitioning to this altered state, unrelenting terror struck once again, grabbed him by the seat of his soul, and shook him from his reverie. As was the case the previous afternoon, a man, clearly visible in great detail with the holiday lighting, and who seemed to be dressed exactly as the first man, went crashing down from the neighboring building across Park Avenue. This time, because the terrace glass door was slightly ajar, he could hear the man's cries of terror. Uncharacteristically, Michael screamed aloud, "Oh my god, noooo—!" Never in his life had he experienced anything as frightening.

Michael was momentarily petrified. The glass of ice water left his paralyzed hand and crashed to the floor. He slowly stood, but didn't move for several moments, and then reluctantly and erratically inched his way out to the terrace. He stopped suddenly, and then shuffled in a stupor across the balcony to the railing.

Fifty-five stories below, there was not a thing out of the ordinary—not one thing! There was an early-morning group of revelers, probably on their way home from an all- night office Christmas party, and New York being the 24/7 city that it is, Park Avenue was still busy with cars and taxis honking their way to who knows where.

His loud scream had awakened Sheila. She came staggering out to the terrace. "Michael, what's wrong?"

He turned to her in a pensive frozen state of fright. "What's wrong? Sheila, didn't you hear his screams?"

"Whose screams, Michael? I only heard yours!"

Michael was present enough to think he might be losing it, but why? He stared starkly at Sheila and then looked back over the railing. "I don't know, Sheila. I have no idea as to what is happening? Perhaps... oh, never mind, I must have had much too much to drink."

"Or, maybe too much of me," she offered with a sulky, sly grin.

"Come on Michael, let's go back to bed and see what happens! Whaddaya say?"

Michael was distraught, but he knew he had to shake this off. And Sheila offered a possible distraction that might be worth a shot. But, probably not.

Chapter 4
Unexplained Past

"The truth is rarely pure and never simple."—**Oscar Wilde**

The next morning Michael left Sheila in bed while she was still dead to the world and he went to see Sophia. She was the only one left in his family and besides Bankei, the only one he could confide in. Sophia would not judge him, nor would she think he was losing it. She understood Michael to the core, and would listen to him as she always did—with empathy, compassion and concern. Her input on challenging matters that Michael faced throughout his life was always much more than helpful and constructive.

A strikingly beautiful widow, Sophia looked at least two decades younger than her 79 years. She had long, flowing, naturally-blond hair with but a hint of gray, deep green eyes and a figure that most 30-year-olds envied. She looked more like Michael's mother than his grandmother; and she had all of the vitality and life philosophies to match her apparent age. "Youthful genes" seemed to run in her family; her mother died at 102 when she looked more like an early-year octogenarian.

Sophia's husband had been a radiation physicist at the Brookhaven National Laboratory on Long Island. Perhaps an occupational hazard; he succumbed to non- Hodgkin's lymphoma two years into their marriage. Subsequently, there had been lots of romantic opportunities, but she never pursued any of them; her husband was her first, last and only love.

Her only child, Barbara, died giving birth to Michael, so Sophia now had no children of her own. She loved Michael selflessly and treated him as if he were her own son. In turn, there was nothing Michael wouldn't do for Sophia. She was his "mom" as well as his confidant all wrapped up in one. He never called her "granny," it was "Sophia" as far back as either of them could recall.

The only impediment between them—Sophia absolutely refused to speak about his father. It wasn't just because he left "cold turkey" when Michael was three years old. Sophia was convinced that her son-in-law Patrick was responsible for Barbara's death. When she went into labor, he was at a "business meeting"—actually, with another woman—and could not be reached on the pager he carried during Barbara's last month of pregnancy. His carnal entertainment apparently caused him to wait much too long to drive her to the hospital. It was no secret that the delivering doctor had the same opinion. At another time and place, there may have been criminal charges brought against Patrick.

Sophia's counsel and support were immensely important when Michael was caring for his dying wife, and simultaneously leading his management team on an international road show to raise funds for his first IPO. He could never have managed both as well as he did without Sophia in his corner. There was nothing he couldn't share with her. She was always there for him, no matter what.

As Michael described what happened at his condo on the prior afternoon, he saw an unexpected strain of anguish rapidly developing on Sophia's face.

"Sophia, what is it?"

"Nothing, Michael; I don't want to talk about! I just can't!"

He snapped back, "Are you kidding me? I just saw a man, or maybe two, appear to fall to their deaths yesterday in front of my very eyes, yet there were no bodies on the street. Sophia, if you have important input on this, I need to hear what you're thinking. Am I losing it?"

Sophia got up from the sofa and walked to the window in her living room. She raised her right hand to her slightly parted lips, stared outside with teary eyes and began to cry, trying desperately to hold it in. Michael got up and ran to her, hugging her from behind as she sobbed uncontrollably. "Sophia, my god, what is it? What's wrong? What did I say that brought this on?"

Sophia inhaled deeply and recovered some of her composure. She was silent for several long seconds and then turned abruptly, looking pensively at Michael. "No, Michael, it's not you. You did nothing wrong." She stopped again, looked down at the floor for several seconds and then at Michael. She continued. "I am not sure what's happening at your place on Park Avenue; but there is an incredibly similar event that I will reluctantly share with you."

Sophia struggled to find the right words. "Do you remember when you decided to buy the penthouse on Park Avenue? I tried in every way I knew how to talk you out of it."

"Sure, I do. You felt I was spending too much money and your impression was that the neighborhood wasn't in my character—I guess you felt I was becoming a snob."

"Yes Michael, that's what I implied, but that's not what I *really* had in mind."

Michael was perplexed. "I don't understand what you're saying. Then what *did* you really mean, and what in the world does it have to do with what happened to me yesterday?"

"Oh god, this is so hard for me to bring up. I promised myself I would never ever discuss this with you or with anyone for that matter." Michael was quiet and perplexed. He sat on the sofa and stared at Sophia, not unlike how he often did as a young boy, with a look that was begging for answers. It was a look that Sophia could never dismiss.

13

"Michael, you know the only source of tension ever to come between us has been my defiance and absolute reluctance to speak about your father. All you know is that he left on your third birthday and never came home again. And thank god, you have been somewhat content to leave it at that. Fortunately, for me and for you, you never pushed very hard for more information."

Michael looked at Sophia as though her comment came out of left field. "What in the world are you talking about?"

"Michael, about a month or so after your father disappeared, there was a small blurb in the City section of The New York Times that reported a man had jumped or fell from the roof of a high rise building and the description of the victim provided in the newspaper was eerily similar to that of your father's."

Sophia continued, "I do...not know what got into me, but for two days I couldn't sleep or stop thinking about what I had read in that article. I don't know why, but for some crazy reason, I thought the man might be your father."

Michael shouted, "What are you saying!" He was beside himself.

Sophia implored, "Michael, please, just let me finish." He reluctantly resigned himself to listen, at least for the moment.

"I finally decided to call the police. They registered the case as a suicide and told me that their 'John Doe,' although well dressed, had absolutely no identification on him and he was still in the morgue. The fall had disfigured his face beyond reasonable recognition. They suggested that I call the medical examiner for his thoughts."

By this time, Michael was staring at Sophia in a near stupor, hanging on her every word. *Where was this all going?* He tried to get up to speak, but Sophia put her hands on his shoulders and guided him back down on to the sofa.

"I called the medical examiner and he told me that if I brought him your father's toothbrush or better yet, some hairs I might find in his bathroom, he could do a DNA test that could conclusively determine whether or not the dead man was your father."

Sophia stammered and cried profusely as she almost inaudibly delivered the final outcome. "Michael, I did as the medical examiner suggested—he ... he was your father!"

By then, Michael was livid that Sophia had never told him any of this. "Why have you kept this a secret for so many years?"

Sophia raised her voice, defending herself, "Because your father was wheeling and dealing with disreputable sleazy people—thieves, gangsters, thugs, you name it. I found out quite accidentally that he was using several of his businesses to launder money for them. I didn't want you to be touched and stigmatized by his unsavory past. But I am absolutely positive your father was not one to commit suicide; no, not Patrick. I am convinced he was pushed to his death; probably for crossing one of his gangster friends. I don't really know; but I know he didn't jump. That just wasn't Patrick!"

Michael was dazed and overwhelmed. He jumped up from the sofa and began frantically pacing the room.

"But Michael, there's more. The building he fell from ... " Sophia began to stammer again, " ... it ... it's the one directly across from your condominium. That's why I tried to talk you out of buying it. I have no idea what all this means; but, I'm scared, Michael, very scared."

Michael stopped pacing and sat back down on the sofa. Sophia collapsed next to him as she sobbed uncontrollably. She just could not contain herself, as all of her pent-up emotions came gushing forth. Michael was silent as he stared into space. He slowly, but tenderly put his arm around Sophia. They both sat there for a long time, a very long time in silence.

CHAPTER 5
SOPHIA'S CHOICE

"Remembering that I'll be dead soon is the most important tool I've ever encountered to help me make the big choices in life." —**Steve Jobs**

Michael stayed at Sophia's home and tried his best to comfort her distress brought on by her disclosure and its possible link to his two experiences at his condominium. He also needed to think deeply and carefully about what Sophia had shared with him. *What could it possibly mean? How was it even possible? I mean, logically possible?*

It was the next day before they could muster the emotional energy to discuss what had transpired the prior evening. Finally, over a light dinner that Michael ordered in from a local deli, he broached the subject.

"Look, Sophia, we can't just let this go. I know it's difficult for you, but I need to know much more. I understand my mother died during my birth. It was years before I got over my guilt from thinking I was directly responsible. And now I finally get a glimpse of my father; sure it's not pretty, but I need closure. I need to know who and what he really was. I can't go the rest of my life wondering about my parents and trying to fill in the blanks. You've got to help me."

"Maybe then I can also make some sense of what happened at my condo as well. It's frightening. It's unreal, like nothing I've ever experienced before! At three years old, when all this was happening, was I somehow cognizant of what was going on? Or, is my father's spirit, if there is such a thing, trying to tell me something? It just doesn't add up! There has got to be a *logical* explanation for all of this!"

Still beleaguered with discomfort, Sophia got up from the dinner table and walked to the kitchen sink, staring out the window into her garden. "You know, Michael, in many ways, this has been terribly painful for me. But, on the other hand, I feel like a huge weight has been lifted off my shoulders."

Sophia paused, turned around and looked deep into Michael's eyes. Now she spoke in a voice that was an octave lower, and with an intensity brought on by terrible memories. "I will do my best, but please understand I never liked your father and he despised me. He understood that I knew him for what he was; and it wasn't very pretty. I did my best for your mom's sake; but, after I found Barbara at the end of her ninth month of pregnancy, unconscious on the floor of their home with the phone in her hand, it was clear to me that he was responsible for her subsequent death during labor."

"In desperation, since Barbara couldn't reach Patrick, she called me for help. I immediately called 911 and raced to her place as fast as I could. I walked in just as Patrick arrived home from his so-called meeting. He had lipstick on his collar and a wretched-smelling perfume all over him. It was clear that he didn't answer Barbara's page because he was probably in bed with some tramp."

Sophia choked back tears. Bringing her thoughts back to that day was a devastating experience.

"I never forgave him and I never will; that bastard! He killed my baby! Actually, I hope someone did throw him off that roof and I hope he suffered like hell every second on the way down."

Michael interjected as Sophia took a deep breath.

"Look, I can understand how you feel about my father. I barely remember him, and what little I do was not of a loving relationship. But whoever and whatever he was, he was my father, and I need to know what happened to him. I also need to understand what's been happening on Park Avenue across from my condo. Are the two somehow connected? I just moved in, and I can't go through this again. Even if I were to leave there, I will always carry the fear that it could happen again. I need to know what's going on and I want it gone—now! And then, hopefully, I can put all of this to rest."

Slightly recovered, Sophia slowly, but sincerely offered, "Michael, I will tell you what I know and whatever I can remember, but I'm not sure how much it will help you." Michael hugged her, "Thank you, Sophia, thank you."

If Michael knew what he was about to learn, would he really feel grateful?

CHAPTER 6
FULL DISCLOSURE

"Human salvation demands the divine disclosure of truths surpassing reason."—**Thomas Aquinas**

S ophia took a deep breath and started at the beginning.

"Michael, your mom was smart, clever and a very diligent worker. She was beautiful; you've seen her photos. After graduating from Columbia Law School, she immediately landed a job with Wachtell, Lipton, Rosen & Katz, which as you know is one of the top law firms in New York. She specialized in commercial tax law and moved quickly up in the firm. As beautiful as she was, Barbara was all work and no play, never the party girl."

"On one occasion after winning a $100 million law suit, she was asked by one of the partners to attend the celebration party at the Four Seasons. There she met a number of "high-fliers" and that's where she met your father. I doubt you will recall, you were too young, and I discarded every photo and remnant of him, but he was handsome, charismatic and a real smooth talker. He swept your mom off her feet and after dating for six months, he proposed to her. She accepted and they were married three months later."

"I told Barbara it was a mistake, but she was smitten with him and there was no talking her out of the marriage. You came along nine month and two weeks after the wedding. Maybe that was the reason for the quick marriage; I really don't know. Your mom never wanted to speak about it because she knew how I felt about your father."

"All through Barbara's pregnancy, he was cheating on her like a mad gigolo. She knew it and made excuses for him; not what you would expect from an intelligent, hard- driving lawyer. She was afraid of losing him; he knew it and he used that fact to manipulate her. He was constantly telling her he was a changed man and they would do wonderful things after you were born."

"But the scariest issue showed its face one afternoon during her sixth month of pregnancy. Barbara was having a challenging time; she was constantly exhausted. That day she called and asked me to come to her place for some help and company. After working all day in her garden, she finally fell asleep upstairs in the bedroom. I dozed off on the sofa in the den just off the living room."

"I was awakened suddenly when I heard men's voices arguing intensely in the living room. Not having slept well the night before, I was really out of it. I at first thought I was dreaming. I immediately noticed your father's voice. I was about to tell him not to make any noise that might wake up Barbara, when I heard a deep, husky, frightening voice of a man with a heavy Eastern European accent. He bellowed like a vicious lion and was lecturing your father with a scary intensity. I closed my eyes and pretended to be sleeping. I hoped and prayed that they wouldn't come into the den. I was deathly frightened, Michael."

"That mean character was telling your father that if he didn't deliver the money he owed him within a week, he would make an example of him and it would leave him with a missing appendage! I was scared to death. If you could only have heard his voice and how he was accosting Patrick! He was like a ferocious animal. From their conversation, it was clear to me that your father was laundering money for this thug at one of his businesses in Jersey. From what they said that afternoon, I believe it was the racetrack your father managed."

"Patrick swore that he would have the cash to him within three days. Then they left the house without disturbing Barbara or finding me in the den. That's the last I ever heard of the guy, although through a phone call I subsequently answered while at Patrick and Barbara's home, I eventually determined that his name was Ivan Prostor. I didn't want to know any more. I never told your mother. While she was pregnant that would have been too much for her to handle."

Michael was in pain, yet grateful for finally knowing the truth about his father, the truth that Sophia had carried all these years locked up in her heart—for his benefit. He dried her tears, hugged her with sincere compassion, empathy and concern as he always did when she was sad, and then softly smiled, "Thanks, Sophia; thank you very much. I know this has been very painful for you ... I'll take it from here."

Jolted by Michael's last comment, Sophia snapped back, "You'll take it from here! What in the world does that mean?"

Michael, deep in thought, gazed at her and said nothing; his wheels were turning in a way they never moved before; where they might lead him, he had no idea— absolutely none. What he did know, and very clearly so, was that he was frightened by the direction they were pointing.

CHAPTER 7
THE MASTER

"Since everything is a reflection of your mind, everything can be changed by your mind."—**Gautama Buddha**

Only one person could help Michael understand and face the demon rising up within his soul—Bankei. Sophia was Michael's confidant and provided the familial warmth he needed in times of crisis. But only Bankei had privy to the very depths of his spirit and possessed the experience and wisdom to deal with major issues of consciousness.

Bankei lived in a small, modest, scantly-decorated apartment above his dojo in Jamaica, in the middle-class borough of Queens in New York City. After Michael's first IPO, being flush with cash, he often earnestly and generously offered to fund Bankei's move to Manhattan. The banter between them was always the same. In typical Indian humor, he suggested Michel was too lazy to make the ride to Queens. Michael always responded that was not the case.

He wanted Bankei to have easy access to well-healed corporate executives who could make a big difference in this world if Bankei could just touch them with his Eastern wisdom. Bankei would always close the discussion with, "As you know, Michael, it was your Jesus who taught that 'It is easier for a camel to go through the eye of a needle than for someone who is rich to enter the kingdom of God.'"

Michael would then respond, "So, I guess the gates of heaven are closed to me. Right?"

"Not at all, Michael. You just have to work harder to get through them. What Jesus was saying is true. Heaven is here and now, right here on Earth. It can be reached inside you, not outside in your five-sense world, and not up in the sky on some lofty cloud or at the edge of the universe. What Jesus was saying is that wealth almost inevitably requires time and emotional energy to manage, so much so that most wealthy people take little or no time to go inside and discover what is infinitely more pleasurable than money and other financial assets. If only they had but a minuscule taste of enlightenment, they would walk away from wealth and power. Their worldly benefits pale in comparison to personal *Ananda*, or should I say bliss."

Michael smiled every time he thought about their good-natured repartee on the subject. Experiencing the burden of overseeing his $250 million fortune, he knew Bankei was right. That was part of the reason he was going to give much of it away.

Michael struggled with the road construction and traffic as he drove to Bankei's apartment on 129th Street, a few blocks off the Van Wyck Expressway. He had arranged the meeting, but did not disclose the subject. He wanted to do that in person. He parked in front of the dojo and noticed no activity so he rang the bell to Bankei's apartment. Nearly five minutes went by and there was no response. Michael was about to call him on his cell phone, when Bankei opened the door.

"Michael, Michael, namaste! Come in, come in."

"Namaste, *Sensei*."

As they walked up the stairs, Bankei continued, "So great to see you! Sorry it took so long to respond. I was on the phone with a student who is desperate for advice on a personal matter; I didn't want to end my call too abruptly with her."

"I understand, not a problem. Welcome back from India. I hope it was an inspiring visit."

"Come Michael; sit here on this cushion while I bring some freshly-bought and freshly-brewed Indian chai."

Bankei scooted off to the kitchen which was only several feet away. As he returned with the tea, he continued, "The trip was magnificent; I had the special opportunity to accompany my cousin, Devi. He lives in Philadelphia, was born in the U.S. and had never been to India."

"Where did you take him?"

"Oh Michael, everywhere, but the highlight of our trip was our three days in the foothills of the Himalayas in Haridwar. As I discussed with you many years ago, it is an eternal spiritual destination for Hindus and among the seven holiest places in India. Although I'm a Buddhist, I still feel the spiritual energy in that city. It is so rich in religious and cultural heritage. Hindu mythology maintains that it was blessed by the three gods, Lord Shiva, Brahma and Vishnu; very much like your Christian Holy Trinity."

"Actually some scholars believe that Jesus traveled to Tibet and India during his 'lost years,' ages 12 through 29, when nothing is disclosed in the bible about his whereabouts. Their sense is that he immersed himself in the teachings of the Eastern Wisdom Seekers and that's why there are many similarities today between Buddhism, Hinduism and Christianity. But that's a whole other story of its own."

"While we were in Haridwar, we managed a number of special attractions: Jai Ganga Maa Har Ki Pauri which is the famous ghat with those blessed steps on the banks of the Ganges River; Mansa Devi, a temple dedicated to the goddess Mansa Devi; and of course, the Maya Devi Temple, which sits on the birth spot of Gautama Buddha. We went to Haridwar this year as next year the Kumbh Mela Festival takes place there. It's conducted once every 12 years and draws millions of people, who come to bathe in the Ganges to wash their sins away. We didn't want to negotiate the masses of visitors during the festival."

"But Michael, you didn't come here to hear me reminisce over my visit to India. What is it that I can do for you, my dearest friend?"

Michael proceeded to explain in great detail the events that took place across from his condo and the revelation he had from Sophia concerning his father's past and falling to his death from the same building 27 years ago.

Bankei looked at Michael for a time and then asked, "Why is it Michael that we have never discussed your father over all these years?"

"Why would we? There's not much to say. I never knew him; he left me when I was three years old."

"And how do you feel about that?"

Silence.

Michael stared at Bankei, and then at the floor. "I really don't know *Sensei*. And I know that I should."

"Michael, I believe there are two forces knocking at the door to your spirit at this time. And, you must face them directly just as Lord Krishna counseled Arjuna in *Bhagavad Gita* in *The Mahabharata* epic."

Michael went to speak, but Bankei held up his hand and an invisible force caused him to stop and listen.

"In the past, we have come close to the discussion we are about to have, and each time you thwarted it off as unnecessary and inconsequential. But this time, you have stepped over a line and I recommend that we proceed."

Michael lifted his gaze from the floor and looked sincerely at Bankei, "I understand and I agree."

Bankei, quiet for a few seconds, shifted to a deep sense of solitude and focus and then began.

"So, let us face the first force. The second will be easy once you recall several lessons we had many years ago."

"Michael, do you remember the Harvard Club Alumni dinner in Hillsborough, California you attended a number of years ago where Steve Jobs was the guest speaker?"

"Sure. Why?"

"You told me you sat next to him at dinner and that you were impressed with his intellect and vision, but you sensed a deep spiritual flaw. When you asked him about his personal life, especially his early upbringing, you said he became arrogant, defensive and intense. You told me you were convinced he had a deep insecurity for being abandoned for adoption by his birth parents. Your emphasis was particularly focused on his biological father, whom Jobs later learned to be a Syrian-American university professor, Abdulfattah John Jandali. Do you know why you focused on his father, Michael?"

Michael said nothing. But he knew why.

"Like Jobs, you feel abandoned. And like him, you have never wanted to face up to this fact. He unfortunately went to his grave never having dealt with the issue. Even more challenging for you from what you have disclosed today, your father was apparently involved in illegal activities, and he may have died because of them."

"On one hand, you want to distance yourself from your father; on the other, you desperately want to have known him personally. You think, *Maybe things could have been different if he raised me. Maybe there was a good side to him.* But you don't know that, and you never will. Things are the way they are because that is the way they are supposed to be. Nothing in the universe that occurs is *illogical* or *unfortunate*. It is because it must be to maintain the balance of universal karma."

"You must find the means to forgive your father and release your anger; you must not judge him. And you know how to do this, Michael. Long ago, I taught you the path to high levels of consciousness. If you like, we can enter that transition together—today."

Michael took a last sip of tea, stood up and bowed before Bankei, "I agree."

He changed into a loose-fitting robe and sat with Bankei in front of an incense- adorned statue of Buddha in Bankei's meditation room. They were about to enter into a practice developed millennia ago by a Buddhist saint in India. It required about three hours of intense focus, and was usually led by a Buddhist

Master. However, once this discipline was learned, it could accomplish in a few hours what might normally require months of psychotherapy.

Because it began with a strenuous series of *pranayama* deep breathing exercises, it is very dangerous unless managed in the presence of a trained expert. Executed incorrectly could lead to brain damage, stroke and death. With Bankei's supervision, Michael had only done this once before, when his wife died, and he could not rid himself of his anger toward *Cosmic Consciousness*, and the universe in general.

During the first hour, Bankei brought Michael to a deep level of altered consciousness. Then, in a rapid *pranayama* exercise, asked him to release his toxic energies by envisioning them as a black smoke exiting his mouth.

For the next two hours, Bankei, using a form of *hypnosis-meditation*, asked Michael to envision his father as best he could and to tell him that although he did not agree with his values, he forgave him, and in fact, held love in his heart for him. This message was repeated over and over again in various formats.

When it was over, Bankei brought them both back to the physical presence of their five senses. Michael's robe was drenched with sweat. As he opened his eyes, at first he could not speak, and then he began to weep like a child, recognizing that his anger towards his father, which had now evaporated, was so misplaced.

Bankei embraced him as if he were his own son. He held him for a long time until Michael was again fully present in the NOW.

Although Bankei was a highly-recognized Buddhist Master, he was not a monk. However, he never married and along the way became an excellent macrobiotic chef. He loved to cook, so he invited Michael to stay for dinner. Michael accepted. He knew how incredibly tasty and healthy his dishes were. While Michael perused the large number of photos from the trip to India, Bankei prepared dinner.

It started with orange and squash soup with lemon polenta croutons and cream. The main course was white fish in a creamy dill sauce with cous cous, peas, carrots and broccoli topped with a lemon-lime dressing. Dessert was a baked pear stuffed with a tahini-miso filling.

"*Sensei,* that was a fantastic meal, and I feel *fantastic.* Thank you for what you've done for me today."

"It's been my pleasure, Michael. But, you will recall I said there were two forces knocking at the door to your spirit."

"Yes, my dear friend. What is the other one?"

"Michael, I have one word for you and with a few moments thought, I am sure you will understand the nature of that force and how it relates to what's happened to you at your condominium."

"I am all ears, *Sensei,* please."

Bankei looked at Michael with a slight but noticeable grin, "Akasha!"

Michael registered the word; he knew what it was; he thought for a moment and then burst with surprise, "Of course, of course! Why didn't I think of it?"

"Because Michael you were strangled by your anger towards your father. But now you're free of that."

Michael was so elated; he almost lost focus on Bankei. He kept quietly repeating, "Akasha... Akasha... Akasha. That must be the answer!"

CHAPTER 8

AKASHA

"Every action in our lives touches on some chord that will vibrate in eternity."—**Edwin Hubbell Chapin**

Michael stayed at Sophia's home that evening; there was still more to discuss so they could reach a common ground of understanding as to what was transpiring in both their lives. He could barely sleep, tossing and turning as he continuously replayed what she had told him, trying to make some sense of it all, and its connection to the one word of wisdom from Bankei—*Akasha*.

Somewhere around 4:00 a.m., as he started to close his eyes, Michael entered a deepening state of altered consciousness, a place he often went to, to untangle challenging issues he faced throughout his life. He called it *meditative reverie*. It was always time well spent. In the wee hours of the early morning, based on his discussions with Bankei and Sophia, he had a thought, one that could explain what was happening across from his condo. As for the connection with Ivan Prostor, that was another matter—or was it?

Over breakfast that morning, Michael decided to share his thoughts with Sophia.

"Sophia, I appreciate your complete openness last evening. Sure, it's been a real eye-opener; but it's been very helpful for me. Eventually, I am sure it will be healing for both of us. I also look at it this way; now there's no longer anything left unsaid between us—and that's good for both of us."

"I agree, Michael. As I said, yesterday, although this has been very painful for me, I feel as though a heavy burden has been lifted from my shoulders."

Michael took a deep breath. "I want to share with you a possibility as to what I may have experienced at my condo, and connect it to what you told me last evening. I came to this possibility after a lengthy discussion and meditation with Bankei. But, I need you to open your mind for this. At least give it your consideration."

Sophia sensed that metaphysical demeanor and look in his eyes. She had seen it many times before as he matured from an anxious young teen into a man.

"Michael, I hope this is not one of your mystical manifestos. You know I have always respected your commitment to mindfulness and Eastern Philosophy. It's just not something I relate to. It always seems to result in *illogical*—no, scratch that—*non-logical* explanations I find difficult to understand and accept."

"Sophia, please here me out. And yes, my explanation is somewhat 'out there.' But with advances that have been made over the past several years in quantum physics, neurology and cosmology, it's the kind of mysticism that's getting closer to a *logical* scientific explanation. And no, I'm not going to throw a pile of equations at you. I wouldn't know how; that's not my forte. Just bear with me, okay?"

"Go ahead, Michael, I'm sorry; I'm all ears."

Michael got up from the breakfast table, walked to the window and stared outside for some time to compose his thoughts. He turned around and looked intently at Sophia and asked, "Have you ever heard of the *Akashic Field*?"

"No, never. What is it and what does it have to do with what we discussed last evening?"

"Maybe everything, maybe everything."

And with that Michael began to explain as best he could in non-technical terms what he had learned over the years about the *Akashic* Field.

"You see, some of the discoveries that are currently being made in quantum physics and cosmology were already known over 5,000 years ago to the Ancient Wisdom Seekers, primarily in India, but also in other parts of Asia. Now, you might ask, 'How in the world is that possible?' I believe if you could go backwards in time and were to ask these wise seekers, they would likely say that *all* wisdom already exists and can be readily accessed. But to do so, you must know how to go *inside* to your *conscious self* and not *outside* to your so-called five-sense physical world, which we are slowly but surely finding is not our true reality."

Sophia was listening carefully, but was not at all convinced. "That sounds nice, but can you give an example of just one piece of knowledge from these wise seekers that has been verified by modern science."

"Okay, I will. But I do want to get to the *Akashic* Field because that's what I believe is behind what's going on here."

Michael continued, "Let me tell you about *entanglement*, something the Ancient Wisdom Seekers were knowledgeable of thousands of years ago, and yet quantum physicists are just beginning to understand."

Sophia was doubtful this would lead anywhere, but she let Michael continue without interrupting his chain of thought.

"You see, if two small particles, say two atoms or molecules, have ever been in close proximity to each other—proximity is *the* key requirement—and then are separated by large distances, even galaxies apart, should one of them experience a change, the other 'knows' it instantly and reacts accordingly—instantaneously, faster than the speed of light! Physicists like to say this occurs *superluminally* fast. The particles are connected by some yet unknown invisible force. In a sense they are *conscious* of each other and any changes that may occur. And yes, the Ancients thought in terms of atoms, although they used a different name. Furthermore, they maintained that since this can occur with atoms, and since everything—you, me, clouds, mountains, oceans, planets and stars—is made up of atoms, then everything must be connected by this invisible force, provided the substance of everything was once in close proximity. And it was. Let me explain."

"These ancient philosophers postulated the *Big Bang* birth of the universe several millennia before modern cosmologists described the same concept. It was "rediscovered" in 1964 when Arno Penzias and Robert Wilson of Bell Labs detected radio waves emitted by celestial objects. These radio waves led to the discovery of the Cosmic Microwave Background, which is relic radiation left over from the formation of the universe via the *Big Bang* expansion."

"For their discovery, Penzias and Wilson shared the 1978 Nobel Prize in physics. Based on their work, we now acknowledge that the universe was created some 13.82 billion years ago in a *Big Bang* by an indescribable fiery expansion within the infinity of nothingness, of the smallest sphere imaginable—physicists call it a singularity. This expansion formed the current universe. Amazingly, all of the energy, matter and information that would ever exist in our universe were contained in that microscopic sphere. That means the requirement of *close proximity* was satisfied and therefore *entanglement* is present everywhere throughout our universe. Everything in the universe is connected—mountains, clouds, oceans, animals, plants and people—everything! Over the last several years, scientists in several laboratories throughout the world have experimentally confirmed the existence of *entanglement*."

"As an aside, the Ancient Seekers' concept of the fate of the universe disagrees with most modern cosmologists, who postulate it will continue to expand for billions of years until all its energy is dissipated and it becomes a black, cold, desolate and lifeless entity. The Ancients, on the other hand, predicted the universe will expand for billions of years and eventually this expansion will slow down and the universe will reverse and then begin to contract on to itself over another period of billions of years, ultimately reforming the initial singularity in what can be referred to as *The Big Crunch*."

"The Ancients posited that the new singularity would again expand in a *Big Bang* event. They believed this cyclic process of arising and subsiding of the universe will occur for eternity, universe after universe after universe, with each cycle creating higher levels of Cosmic Consciousness in the new constituents. A few highly-regarded physicists believe in this model. They call it *The Big Bounce*—small bubbles of a new universe being born, expanding to a large ball, then contracting back to the small ball, bouncing for eternity breeding-expanding-deflating-then breeding again."

"Goodness! Michael, this is all very interesting, but you're beginning to lose me. Are you telling me that everything in the universe is connected? Is there any simple proof of this connectivity above and beyond this entanglement idea?"

"Okay, here's an example. There is an initiative called the Global Consciousness Project that grew out of a decades-long program at Princeton University. Scientists there demonstrated with high statistical significance that research subjects who focused their mental energy or awareness on a simple machine called a random number generator were able to cause its output to deviate from its normal random listing of numbers to a list with a preordained order. That is to say, some level of order was created in the numbers emanating from the machine. Normally, the order of numbers would be completely random."

"This finding eventually grew into the Global Consciousness Project. For nearly 20 years, this group has had 70 random number generators operating at host sites around the world. When a significant global event such as 911 in Manhattan has occurred, they measure a structured output that could never have formed randomly; the chance of such occurrence is less than one in a trillion. They feel this demonstrates a connection of consciousness among the billions of people on the planet who become aware of such an event, and in some way are emotionally affected by it."

Michael could see Sophia's eyes beginning to glaze over, so he went right to the main message he wanted to leave with her. "Sophia, please bear with me for just a few minutes longer. What do you say?"

She actually managed a touch of humor. "Okay, I'll pinch myself to stay awake! Just kidding! Please go ahead, I'm with you, promise."

"Thanks!"

"You see, this connectivity is very much related to a concept that the ancient Hindu Seekers called *Akasha*, meaning 'open air' or 'space'. It is a Sanskrit word that Ervin Laszlo, a well-known international systems scientist calls the *Akasha Paradigm* or *Akashic Field*. He believes, as did the Ancient Wisdom Seekers every action that has every happened since the beginning of the universe is recorded in this field, and that anyone in the proper state of consciousness can access this information. In fact, if you become adept at tapping into the *Akashic Field* in a kind of *quantum communion* with this universal oneness, you can achieve phenomena that we consider supernatural, but to the Ancients were quite natural—clairvoyance, spiritual healing, levitation and much more."

"Basically, Laszlo is underscoring that we are living in a conscious universe, and we are part of that consciousness. By properly connecting with the *Akashic Field*, it is possible to vividly experience and even visualize with your five senses, events that happened in the past, even thousands of years ago!"

"I have studied a number of ancient texts concerning the *Akasha*, as well as several of Laszlo's well-documented books on the subject. I believe that the *Akashic Field* may be responsible for *hyperthymesia*, a condition observed in some autistic patients. *Thymesia* is the Greek word for 'memory.' *Hyperthymestics* can recall in great detail vast amounts of their life experiences. People with this syndrome also have an unusual form of what is known as *eidetic* memory. They can remember and instantly recall from their past in a perfectly organized manner, all of the trivial details of specific personal events, including the date, the weather and what people were wearing on that day. For some, their recall goes back to the womb and beyond!"

"It seems that certain forms of autism may induce this unique ability. These individuals can plug into the *Akashic Field* and visualize all that has ever happened to them in great detail. In instances of autistic savants, they may also visualize information from past events created by others, and this may be the source of their great intellectual capabilities. Can you imagine an average non-scientist person, who has learned the skills to access higher levels of consciousness, connecting to the *Akashic Field* and being able to use Einstein's equations to solve problems in General Relativity!"

Michael was now on a roll with a subject that was close to his heart. "There is another reason the Ancients were interested in the *Akasha*. They believed that the past, as recorded in the *Akashic Field* and the present form the entire structure of human-kind. In other words, we carry all of the information from our past and our present, and any alteration of this content results in an alteration of our present and our future. They believed that it was possible to revise the records of your past in the *Akashic Field*, and thereby affect your present and future."

Michael wanted to validate his point with scientific cred-ibility. "You're absolutely correct if you think that mainstream science is skeptical of these ideas. But, I can tell you that in addi-tion to Ervin Laszlo, a number of other highly respected scien-tists including world-renowned physicists David Bohm, Freeman Dyson and Fritjof Capra have discussed and strongly support the concept that the universe is in fact conscious. Some of these sci-entists feel this consciousness emanates from, or possibly is part of what is called by physicists, the quantum vacuum or zero-point energy."

"Wow, Michael! That's a lot to swallow in one gulp! So, are you saying that your father falling off that roof was recorded in this *Akashic Field* and that somehow you "tuned in" to this information and saw it replayed in your mind's eye?"

"Precisely!"

"That all sounds like smoke and mirrors to me!"

"Look Sophia, over the years, I have spent numerous hours in deep meditation; and throughout the day, I often drift into what I call *meditative reverie*, where my eyes may even be open, but I have shifted to an altered state of consciousness. I have found this a very effective means to ponder and understand difficult ideas, and a wonderful way to increase my creative thought process through mindfulness."

"So, do you think you were in such a state when these two events of falling men appeared before your eyes and that somehow at those very moments you were plugged into this so-called *Akashic Field*?"

"Exactly! I think it's a good possibility. In both instances, I was staring across from my condo, lost in meditative reverie, and I extracted these events into my mind's eye from the *Akashic Field*."

Sophia was struggling to understand what Michael was sharing with her. She gave it some credence because it came from him, but it was a bit much for her to fathom at the moment.

"Well Michael, considering all other options, of which I know none, and considering how solid I know you are emotionally, I will certainly give this some serious thought. These are challenging ideas for me. But, who knows, Michael? Who knows?"

CHAPTER 9

DINNER WITH IVAN

"Appear weak when you are strong and strong when you are weak."—**Sun Tzu**, **The Art of War**

You don't have the success of a Michael Pierce and not have been in touch with some of the most powerful and "connected" people in business and politics. Michael was an unusual CEO in an increasingly competitive world. He was well-liked, even admired for an unusual mix of genius, integrity, fairness and thoughtfulness. Perhaps, this was because of his personal dedication to share his companies' successes with *all* of their *stakeholders*—employees, customers, shareholders, suppliers, community, and of course, the world.

His ventures and personal vision always had a solid mission and focus to make a positive difference for the greater good. The emotional and financial returns were generally significant for all of these stakeholders, and they never forgot his commitment to them. Michael set out to tap into this network to find out: *Who was Ivan Prostor? What kind of person was he? What was his game? Was he still alive, and if so, where was he?*

It didn't take too long to find out that Prostor was a Russian immigrant mobster, now in his mid-sixties, living in Brooklyn. Many years ago, he had built a local empire in loan-sharking, drugs, prostitution and the numbers racket. He had been brought up on criminal charges several times, but was never convicted; a combination of excellent legal representation and payoffs to the right people.

But Ivan was a greedy man, and not very thoughtful in how he wielded his power. He was eventually shut down by the New York Mafia families for not playing by their rules, and was actually lucky to be alive. It was rumored that Ivan had paid off the New York families more than $5 million in hard clean cash to settle their grievances, and in fact, to stay alive. He was forced to turn over all of his businesses to them and forgo any further operations in the New York and New Jersey area. It was a real awakening for Ivan, but he valued his life and still had enough money to live the good life well into the future.

The deal was brokered for Ivan by Mario Luciano, a distant cousin of the infamous Sicilian mafia boss, Lucky Luciano, and a member of the Columbo La Cosa Nostra family. Ivan had done lots of favors for Mario over the years, and fortunately for Ivan, they saved him from a very brutal ending. By all rights, he should have been sleeping with the fish in the sea.

With lots of cash still stashed away in several numbered accounts in Switzerland, Ivan now found his kicks at the racetrack and with pretty young ladies. He lived alone at his home in Brooklyn Heights. His first and only wife died under mysterious circumstances when she drowned in their indoor swimming pool. She was a descendant of a Russian aristocratic family from St. Petersburg, wealthy in her own right. So Ivan also had a major inheritance to supplement the huge Swiss store of cash from his prior illegal businesses. His wife's body was cremated before an autopsy could be considered. There was no investigation, nor were any charges brought against Ivan. As usual, he paid off the right people.

But Ivan's karma had come back to visit him and he began to pay his dues. He had contracted a rare neurological disease and was now ambulatory with a cane, but more often than not, in a wheelchair. However, that didn't stop him from seeking and enjoying the "good life." Parties, the racetrack and young girls;

they were still his thing, even in "retirement." Actually, his party pace had increased over the last couple of years, as though he knew there were not many left.

Michael decided to meet Ivan Prostor. He wasn't quite sure of all the details, but he knew he had to do it. *Who was this guy, who may have killed his father?* Perhaps, he would finally learn more about his father and what actually happened, which was the key driving force for him.

He put a private detective on Ivan and learned that he went to De Benedetto's for lunch nearly every Friday. An upscale Italian restaurant, not far from his home in Brooklyn Heights, De Benedetto's specialized in Sicilian dishes. Apparently, Ivan had a thing for good southern Italian food.

Michael loved Italian food too, so why not? He reserved a table the following Friday under the name Michael Carlotti. He had the look, had studied the language at NYU, and even spent a semester in Rome as part of an exchange program where he learned to speak Italian.

To play his part well, Michael hired a driver with a new shiny black Rolls Royce limo to chauffeur him to the restaurant. Dressed to the nines in a midnight blue Brioni suit, a tailored silk white shirt, blue and white Ferragamo tie, white silk pocket handkerchief, Missoni patent leather shoes and custom sunglasses, Michael entered De Benedetto's. He was warmly greeted by Antonio, the maître d', who looked the part for an authentic Italian restaurant; slim build, mid-50s, slightly bald salt and pepper hair, chevron mustache, Roman nose, and all of the intensity that could instantly cycle between exhilaration and chaos.

"Bongiorno, bongiorno, Señor!"

"Bongiorno, I'm Michael Carlotti. I booked a table for one for lunch."

"Si, Señor Carlotti; how about that booth over there, overlooking the river and the beautiful Brooklyn bridge?"

"Si, quello a buono!"

Antonio smiled at Michael's perfect accent and pronunciation.

As he strolled to the booth, Michael heard the deep scratchy voice of a man seated two tables away in a wheelchair. It was definitely Eastern European. It had to be Prostor. The man bellowed with a volume and animation, as if he were the restaurant owner.

"Antonio, this branzino is overcooked. Take it back and get me a new main course, and tell that chef of yours he'd better get it right this time. And don't take all day. I've got a doctor's appointment in a couple of hours and I don't want to be late! Capish?"

"Si, Señor Prostor. Please have a glass of your favorite Pinot Grigio on me while you're waiting."

"I'll have more than Pinot Grigio on you if you don't move your ass and get me my fish!"

"Si si, Señor Prostor; subito, subito!"

Although confined to a wheelchair, Prostor did not at all appear feeble. With a hefty 200-plus pound frame, he was impeccably dressed in a black double-breasted suit, a bright pink French-cuffed shirt and a lavender and white, silk, striped tie. Well tanned for the winter months, he sported a large diamond pinky-ring, had well manicured nails and a full head of thick, wavy, completely white slicked-back hair. His impenetrable eyes and inscrutable countenance gave very little semblance of the potential terror inside, but his deep raspy voice said it all. You did not ever want to cross Ivan.

There were only two other tables occupied besides Prostor's and Michael's; an older gentleman, who was sleeping over his wine and a young couple, too engaged in their flirtatious actions to hear anything. And both were quite a distance away on the other side of the restaurant.

Prostor eyed Michael and knew by his looks and dress he must be a man of means. He stared at Michael for a few seconds and then complained, "You know, I've been coming to this dump for over 10 years. The wine and food's good, but the service— ahh, they never get it perfect, and I hate imperfection! You know what I mean?"

To put Ivan a bit off guard, Michael used a stress-inducing technique he had learned years ago from Bankei. Michael looked straight into Prostor's right eye, waited three long seconds before responding slowly and coolly, "I understand. But, you know, Antonio may do better if he wasn't operating under fear."

"What the hell is that supposed to mean?"

Michael continued staring at Ivan's right eye. "Did you see how his hands were shaking when he took your plate and brought your wine?"

"So what! For years I made a good living by keeping people in fear; you know what I mean?"

Michael ended his stark stare and broke into a gentle smile. "Sure, I agree there may be times and places where that's necessary, but here in this restaurant, these guys are like timid artists. Their creativity folds up under fear. I think you would get much more out of the chef and Antonio, if they weren't operating as if they had a gun to their head."

Prostor took in a deep breath, rolled his eyes, exhaled staring for just a moment at the ceiling, swallowed a large gulp of Pinot Grigio and then looked at Michael. "Well, maybe you have a point. Let me think on it. Anyway, what's your name?"

"Michael Carlotti, and yours?"

"Ivanović Prostor. You can call me Ivan."

"Nice to meet you, Ivan." Michael pronounced it in proper Russian. Ivan smiled. He was impressed by Michael's knowledge of the Russian language.

Antonio was standing erect in a nervous stance at Michael's table, a bead of sweat swiveled its way from the top of his forehead into the eyebrow over his left eye. He didn't move to wipe it. When the conversation between Ivan and Michael took a five second intermission, he stammered, "Señor Carlotti, whenever you're ready, I ... uh ... take ... uh ... your order."

Michael turned to him and addressed him with a sincere smile, "Antonio, how long have you been working here?"

"Señor, about 22 years."

"You must be very good for the owner to keep you on that long, right?"

"Ma, Señor, I...uh... don't know. I guess so."

"Don't be modest, Antonio. I can see the way you're working that you know the ropes. So I want you to do me favor. Just relax and enjoy your day. I think it would be a much better day for everyone, including you Antonio, if there was a lot less stress between here and the kitchen. What do you think?"

Antonio looked at him at first perplexed, but then with an authentic smile. "Si, Señor."

"Now, please bring me your melanzana alla parmigiana, and a side of fresh spinach, lightly sautéed with garlic and olive oil. I will also take a bottle of your 1986

Brunello di Montalcino."

"Si Señor; subito!" Antonio ran off to the kitchen with a huge smile on his face.

Ivan had been watching this with a touch of fascination. "Very nice, Michael. Let's see how that melanzana and spinach come out. I can vouch for the Brunello, it's one of my favorites."

As lunch progressed, Ivan and Michael found themselves in occasional conversation. You could see that Ivan was trying to determine Michael's story, but Michael was too astute for that. Ivan learned very little, and certainly nothing that would disclose Michael's true identity.

Michael finished with a longo espresso. He thanked Antonio for a great lunch and excellent service. He paid the bill in cash and left Antonio a generous tip, complemented by the rest of his Brunello.

"Antonio, I only had one glass of that marvelous Brunello. It would be a shame to see it go to waste. The rest is all yours. Take it home. I insist!"

Antonio raised his eyebrows in a bit of astonishment, "Grazie Mille, Señor Carlotti!"

Ivan had been watching Michael with interest all during lunch. "Hope to see you again, Michael."

"Great, Ivan, enjoy the rest of your day!" Michael moved slowly to the restaurant entrance with Ivan stealthily following behind at a distance in his wheelchair. After the door closed behind Michael, Ivan sat in his wheelchair peering out the window at Michael and his swank transportation.

As the driver opened the back door to the Rolls Royce and Michael stepped in, you could see the wheels turning in Ivan's mind. Mostly lots of questions. He had to get to know this guy. Ivan thought quietly under his breath, "He's a guy with lots of class."

As the limo pulled away, Michael smiled and thought to himself... *I've got him!*

CHAPTER 10
THE CON

"The devil's finest trick is to persuade you that he does not exist."—**Charles Baudelaire**

Every Friday for the next few weeks, Michael had lunch at De Benedetto's, and each time he moved a little bit closer to Ivan Prostor. Ironically, it was Friday the 13th, three days before Ivan's 65th birthday, when he planned to set things right with him; whatever that meant, he still wasn't sure. They dined together at De Benedetto's. Ivan was his guest-of-honor for a special celebration for his upcoming birthday. Michael ordered a bottle of 2004 Chateau Petrus for $2,000. He arranged with Antonio to buy the bottle beforehand, as it wasn't something they stocked at De Benedetto's.

Michael knew that Antonio would likely disclose this information to Ivan. And sure enough, "Mamma mia! Señor Prostor, he must really like you, he asked me to order a $2,000 bottle of Chateau Petrus for your birthday lunch together!"

"What an incredible guy, that Michael! He's the only one I've met in years who is truly worthy of my trust."

"Si, Señor Prostor, I completely agree. He's very special, a real prince!"

Michael's flare and appreciation for elegant wines, gourmet food and excellent service served him well in preparing for Ivan's feast. He arrived early for the lunch, adirected Antonio to set the table in a way that was fit for a king. He had also paid the owner a generous sum for exclusive use of the restaurant for their lunch celebration. From a luxury caterer, Michael had arranged for Antonio to rent Baccarat crystal, Royal Worcester China and Royal Doulton flatware all set on Sferra Classico Italian linen. It was a $10,000 meal even before the food arrived at the table!

Ivan was impressed beyond all expectations. No one had ever done anything close to this for him, especially when not asking for something in return. What did he do to deserve such adoration and recognition? With his Russian upbringing and indoctrination, he was not beyond suspicion.

Although difficult for him to speak from his heart, Michael quickly put that to rest. "Look, Ivan, not to worry, I grew up without a father, and I guess in the past few weeks I have found you to be my father figure. I love you, my friend." Michael kissed him on both cheeks, not unlike the infamous Mafioso Boccio della Morte, the kiss of death.

That did it. Ivan was near tears. No one, but no one had ever been so direct and caring of him. Of course he wasn't an easy guy to care for and to reach his soul. But Michael was brilliant and had all of the right skills and experience to do this smoothly and with an unquestionable appearance of genuineness. However, under any other circumstances, this would have been a difficult task, even for Michael.

It was a set menu. Michael had gauged Ivan's tastes by close observation and discussions with him. But he intended to stretch way beyond Ivan's standards, including premium grade Beluga caviar for $250 an ounce, and Stoli Elit: Himalayan Edition vodka at $3,000 a bottle. Such epicurean delights had never before touched De Benedetto's kitchen, or Ivan's taste buds.

The menu started with perfectly created Russian blinis and vodka, followed by pumpkin tortellini laced with crème fraise, farm-raised venison ragu and finely-chopped roasted pistachio nuts. Ivan loved lamb, so the main course was *Agnello Siciliano*. The lamb was flown in from a small ranch in New Zealand that specialized in grain-fed baby lambs that were periodically massaged, not unlike Kobe beef. The meat was marinated in a special "secret" sauce for 48 hours, then lightly grilled and finally stewed for 20 minutes in a rich herbal Arrabiatta tomato sauce made using a recipe from a chef friend of Michael's living in Cammarata, Sicily.

Dessert was based on Sicily's number one favorite—cannoli, but a very special cannoli. The crust was made from unbleached flour, seasoned with fresh mint and cardamom, and formed into a paste with a vintage Chateau Margot wine, before creating the shell and slowly deep-frying it in first-grade sesame seed oil. The filling was created from young goat's milk ricotta, coconut-raspberry coulis and a pinch of Frangelico liquor. Finally, it was slightly flamed at the table with a pinch of 30-year-old Courvoisier brandy. This was truly a feast fit for a king!

During dinner, Ivan was beside himself as Michael elaborated on the source of the recipes and the history attached to each. He studied Ivan throughout the meal and measured his alcohol intake as he and Antonio poured generously. By the meal's end, Ivan was feeling no pain.

Slightly slurring in his deep Russian voice, Ivan pronounced, "Michael, this was the most magnificent meal I have had in my entire 65 years on this miserable planet! Thank you, thank you, thank you!"

"Ivan, it was my pleasure. You are truly a father to me and I plan to learn much from you." He got up from the table and walked over to Ivan, and bent over his wheelchair, kissing him again on both cheeks. Michael felt like Judas Iscariot, but he knew all of this was necessary if he were to find out about his father. There was no other way.

With tears in his eyes, Ivan confessed, "Michael, I appreciate your thoughts, but with this damned disease, who the hell knows how much more time I've got?"

Michael was beginning to feel a sense of sorrow and compassion for this misguided human being. He thought, *how could someone, who has been so involved in the worst of crimes, also have such a soft side. What is really behind this poor misled person?*

"Ivan, life is sweet; don't think that way! You have lots of time left! And to cap off your birthday celebration, I want to share a special closing drink with you. A few years ago, I was at an auction at Harrods in London, and was successful in purchasing a bottle of Courvoisier L'Esprit. It's very old and was owned and blessed personally by Napoleon himself. I have been waiting for the right occasion to open the bottle. And this is truly it!"

And with that Michael unlocked and then reached inside a rich-looking leather box and removed a beautifully engraved crystal flask. He gently opened the glass- stoppered bottle and produced two of the most beautiful Baccarat crystal brandy glasses.

"Ivan, these glasses date back to 1794. I acquired them years ago from an antique dealer in Paris. They're from a collection that was owned by Napoleon Bonaparte. He was said to have drunk from them. Let's do the same. I am confident you and I will find a means to co-mingle our lives in a strategic way that would make even Napoleon envious!" And with that they both imbibed a magical, smooth brandy that cost Michael a healthy four figures in British sterling.

"Michael, you are a man of class! And you know how to spend your wealth to enjoy life to its fullest. I envy you!"

In response, Michael poured a second round of the Napoleonic brandy. However, because of Ivan's "altered state of consciousness," what he did not see was the nearly invisible 0.15 grams of diazepam, a potent sleep-inducing drug that Michael had discretely placed at the bottom of Ivan's glass. With alcohol, the dosage must be accurately controlled; otherwise, it could be deadly. Dorothy Kilgallen, noted journalist and TV game show panelist of the 1950s and 60s, was found dead in her New York townhouse after she mistakenly combined a similar sleep-inducing drug with alcohol.

But Michael had lots of prior experience with this drug. His deceased wife, while fighting cancer, suffered from severe insomnia. Diazepam was the only drug that worked for her, and Michael became an expert at inducing the entire spectrum of altered states of consciousness, from mild drowsiness to a 24-hour deep slumber.

Within 10 minutes, Ivan was slumped over in his wheelchair. Antonio came over and with a smile offered, "Mamma mia, Señor Carlotti! Señor Prostor, he sleeps like a baby; he even has a smile on his face!" Actually, his concave mouth was beginning to dribble on to his shirt.

"Antonio, I have my car here. I'll take him home; it's not a problem at all."

"Gratia Millia, Señor Carlotti!"

With that, Michael paid the bill and gave Antonio a tip that was likely greater than the total sum of all the gratuities he had received over the last two years. Antonio was flabbergasted and beside himself. He helped Michael with Ivan and the wheelchair into the Rolls limo, which had enough space between the front and back seats to fit two wheelchairs.

"Señor Carlotti, you sure I can no help?"

"No, Antonio, it's not a problem at all. I've got it under control."

As he started to drive away, Michael thought, *Antonio, it's not a problem at all—really?* He had no idea what kind of problem was in front of him.

Chapter 11
Ride to Destiny

"The risk of a wrong decision is preferable to the terror of indecision." —**Maimonides**

Before coming to De Benedetto's, Michael had arranged to have the limo without the driver, so that he could attend to Ivan on his own, returning the car later that day. As he drove through Brooklyn towards the bridge, he could hear Ivan snoring as he dribbled away in never-never land.

Michael had a solemn yet intense posture. His mind wandered back and forth from disdain to distraught for the poor soul in the back seat. He had never been in a situation that elicited such negative feelings. He was, in fact, disturbed and frightened by these feelings. What should he do with him? Over the past several weeks, he obsessed about confronting Ivan, but when it came down to it, he didn't have a fixed plan as to what to do with him. After all, this was not Michael's normal business, and he was conflicted by his commitment to live a conscious life. All he knew is that he had to do something, but what that something was, he had no idea. And certainly, not before he learned more about his father. And yes, he had forgiven his father, but had yet to do so with Ivan.

Michael didn't even contemplate driving to Ivan's house. Guided by his subconscious compass, he headed slowly, but intently across the Brooklyn Bridge, up through SOHO on

Broadway, and without a conscious thought, he found himself in Greenwich Village on Park Avenue South. He progressed very slowly, in continuous thought; so slowly that taxis were honking and cursing him at every other block.

He had to think; what should he do with the "package" in the back seat? Dump him in the East River? He could never do that. Leave him drugged on the streets of Harlem? No. His mind was bouncing like a ball between ghastly scenarios. This wasn't Michael. He was frustrated, torn and for the first time, as long as he could recall, uncertain about how to make an important decision. Furthermore, he had not yet had his ultimate conversation with Ivan, disclosing who he really was and trying to learn what actually did happen to his father? He hoped that some remaining semblance of the mindfulness exercise he went through with Bankei would help in his decision concerning Ivan.

Finally, he was there; Park Avenue in front of the *Tour De Versailles* Condominiums. He was on mental automatic pilot and barely recalled leaving De Benedetto's. Michael drove a few blocks further uptown. Almost without thought, he found himself making a U-turn, driving slowly but intently to that place; the place that had been imprinted, but submerged in his subconscious for weeks; the building across from his condo where his father had "fallen" to his death 27 years before.

Michael drove a few hundred feet beyond the entrance and parked the Rolls in the public car park. He removed a large screwdriver from the toolkit in the trunk and placed it unceremoniously in his breast pocket, and then lifted Ivan and his wheelchair from the back seat. Ivan was still out cold. He removed Ivan's shoelaces and discreetly tied his upper arms snug to the chair, so that he wouldn't fall during his slumbering transport. Very slowly, Michael wheeled him toward the entrance to the building. Moving guardedly, he waited while the doorman helped several people with large packages they were bringing into the lobby.

At just the right moment, Michael deftly maneuvered himself and his passenger past the busy reception area to the express elevator on the far side of the lobby. The elevator was located in a small vestibule around the corner, conveniently away from the hectic holiday activities. It went directly to a French restaurant on the 65th floor, where Michael had been several times before for dinner.

On their way up, Michael could hear an occasional snort from Ivan and a few indistinct Russian words here and there, as if he were arguing with someone in a bad dream. When the doors opened, he carefully peered out in both directions. As expected, the long hallway to the left which curved sharply for quite some distance before reaching the restaurant entrance was quiet. They served only dinner and it was still early. Several feet to his immediate right was a large black door signed with fading white letters, "*Roof.*"

Michael moved quickly. As anticipated when parking the car, the door to the roof was locked. He quietly wheeled Ivan to the side of the door and removed the screwdriver from his jacket. After driving it in with a strong thrust into the latch area, he pried with hefty leverage as he pulled on the doorknob. Nothing; it was stuck. He continued to manipulate the screwdriver, but to no avail.

Suddenly, he heard a distant conversation approaching in the hallway from the restaurant, walking towards the elevator. Michael knew he had perhaps 15 to 20 seconds before the intruders came around the corner, and he and Ivan were discovered. Should he abandon his "plan," whatever that was and take the elevator down, or continue prying the door?

At that moment Michael noticed a large rectangular metal bar sitting on the floor near the lower hinge of the door. It was probably used as a heavy doorstop when carrying things up to the roof. He grabbed it and used it as a hammer to pound viciously at the screwdriver, first deep into the latch and then on the side of the screwdriver handle, trying desperately to wedge the door lock free. The voices grew louder. It was only a matter of seconds before Michael and Ivan would be in plain view.

Suddenly, the door sprung free. Michael quickly wheeled Ivan to the small landing on the other side of the door. He closed it quietly, and almost immediately heard the two restaurant employees at the adjacent elevator door. They were ranting in French and broken English, a vigorous intense argument over salary and their end-of-year bonus.

The elevator bell rang; the door opened. They stepped in and were gone. *Silence.* Michael was home free—at least for the moment.

CHAPTER 12
UP ON THE ROOF

"Seldom, very seldom, does complete truth belong to any human disclosure; seldom can it happen that something is not a little disguised, or a little mistaken." —**Jane Austen**

Michael was strong well beyond his years from a highly disciplined workout program over the last couple of decades. He had little problem pulling hefty Ivan and his wheelchair up twenty-three steps to the roof door. It was unlocked, not a problem at all. He swung open the door and positioned Ivan facing out over the skyline, about 10 feet from the roof ledge. With a 20 degree drainage slope at this point on the roof, Michael had to wedge the large screwdriver under the front wheels of the wheelchair to prevent Ivan from taking a quick trip to the ledge and a plunge to eternity. Not that way. Michael wanted to speak openly with him. He had no intention of physically hurting, much less, killing him. That wasn't Michael.

Time passed slowly for Michael. *I want to get as much truth from Ivan as possible concerning my father and their dealings together.* He had conjured up a plan in his mind as he was parking the Rolls in the garage. *I have a thought as to what to do afterwards, but that will have to come later. Is it really the right way to go? Maybe. But it's a challenging path.* He meditated and sought internal guidance.

It was a long two hours until Ivan began to awake from his drug-induced slumber. His head bobbed from left to right until he reached a somewhat sensible level of consciousness. Ivan knew something wasn't right when he felt his arms tied to his chair.

His first slur was a question, "Michael, what the hell is going on? Where are we?"

Michael stared at him intently as he marched slowly around the wheelchair. "You've been here before, Ivan. Doesn't it look familiar?"

Ivan stared around and knew he was on the roof of a building, but in his current state, he had no recollection of the exact place.

"It was a very long time ago, Ivan, 27 years to be exact."

Still under the influence of alcohol and diazepam, Ivan was foggy and confused. Shaking in his chair like a drunk, he looked alternately at Michael and his surroundings trying to fathom what was happening to him.

Michael raised his voice just short of shouting, "Ivan, look at me! Do I look familiar to you?"

Ivan stared at Michael and then at the roof fixtures around him, "Sure, you're Michael Carlotti. And again, where the hell are we and why are my arms tied to my chair?"

Although he was drugged, even in his current condition, Ivan was still a very savvy individual; he'd "been around the block" more than once. He knew something was wrong, and he didn't like what he felt. "Michael, what's going on, and what do you want from me?"

"Okay, Ivan, I'll give you a hint. The name's not Carlotti; it's Pierce. Familiar to you?"

"Pierce? Who in the hell?" Ivan stared at him, "Pierce … Pierce … Pierce." He strained his brain, but after a minute or so, it hit him like a ton of bricks and he retaliated as if he had instantly sobered up, "You're not related to that bum Patrick Pierce, are you?"

"He was my father, Ivan. And you pushed him off this roof 27 years ago from this very spot. I was only three years old at the time, and never had the chance to get to know him."

Silence.

"What the hell are you talking about? I never pushed anyone off a roof. Are you kidding me?"

"Look at me, Ivan! Look at where we are! Do I look like I'm kidding?"

After a long interlude and the sight of Michael's contorted angry grimace just a few inches from his face, Ivan replied, "Alright, alright, I pushed him off, and yes, from this very spot!"

"But, Michael, Michael, Michael, you are so fortunate. He wasn't a good father. He was a real jerk, a thief. He stole from everyone. He stole from me, once, twice, but the third time that was enough. He had to pay. *It was just business, Michael, just business.*"

"Ivan, you must be kidding me. And who did you steal from, or is that a different ball of wax?"

"Michael, yes, it *is* different. I only stole from weaklings, idiots who could not manage their lives. Michael, I treated your father like a king. I sent him on incredible vacations with beautiful women. I was fine with him and his buddies getting a reasonable percentage on the money they laundered for me and my clients. But when I caught him siphoning funds through his intricate accounting scheme, I had to make an example of him. He was a financial genius, but an inconsiderate fool, a real liability, Michael!"

"What do you mean, siphoning funds?"

"Your father was connected with a number of small businesses in New York and in Jersey, and he used them as part of his laundering scheme. But he thought he was a regular Robin Hood, steal from the rich and give to the poor. Instead of giving me the full amount owed to me after processing my money, he found a clever way to give his cohorts a higher percentage than I had negotiated with him and those dumb cronies. He got away with it for some time until somebody, who didn't think he was getting his fair share, tipped me off. No honor among thieves, Michael."

"Your father felt sorry for these small-time nobodies. He was robbing from me for their benefit. That just ain't right! When I found out, he had to pay. I had to show the others that this kind of underhanded crap was unacceptable. *Michael, it was just business, just business. I swear.*"

"And besides, believe me Michael, your life's been far better off without that disloyal, cheating bastard! Now, untie me and let's discuss this as the friends we really are. Please, Michael."

Michael managed a forced smile. "Sure Ivan, I understand, I'll untie you and we can have that discussion. I would love to know more." With that, Michael untied Ivan, who was still partially drunk and drugged. As he released him from his bondage, Ivan tried desperately and clumsily to stand up out of the chair, but in his present condition, there was no way that could happen. As Michael struggled to keep him seated, he inadvertently kicked the screwdriver holding the front wheels of the wheelchair, and Ivan began to accelerate towards the ledge.

Ivan screamed as loud as he could, "Michael, stop this chair, are you crazy?" Except for the friction of the wheels on the roof surface, the chair accelerated exponentially with each second. That's the way the physics of gravity works.

The chair was now within three feet of the ledge with Ivan helplessly attempting to lift himself from the chair, screaming and cursing in Russian, as Michael ran for the chair to save Ivan from the fall. But something happened on his way to the ledge. Michael's foot stepped hard on the large screwdriver he had earlier unintentionally kicked from the front wheels. The round handle of the screwdriver rolled vigorously under Michael's right shoe, causing him to take a hard fall flat on his back as Ivan and the chair approached the ledge.

The next three seconds happened in what appeared to Michael to be slow motion. The chair with Ivan in it was just inches from smashing into the ledge, which at this section of the roof was a mere 18-inch high retaining wall. Ivan was going over the edge, wheelchair and all.

Michael sprung from the roof floor and dove with everything he had to prevent Ivan's fall. Ivan was screaming incongruently at him, "Please help me, Michael; I'm going over!"

Michael's strong maximally-extended athletic body flew through the air like a well-trained baseball player diving for home plate. His conscious mind was laser focused on a single task, save Ivan. As his outstretched arms reached beyond the wheelchair, he barely caught him. His hands closed like a tight steel vice on to Ivan's jacket. Unfortunately, his head slammed into the retaining wall and he was knocked into a semi- conscious state. He had no idea how long he was in that state, as he began to process Ivan's desperate screams for help.

Michael's hands were still somehow miraculously locked onto the jacket of this 200-pound "bull" of a man. Were it not for the strength in Michael's hands from extensive rock climbing, Ivan would have gone over the edge. He pulled himself to his knees and hauled a precariously perched and deeply frightened Ivan up on to the retaining wall. For who knows how long, Ivan had been staring straight down at the view 65 floors below him. And now there Ivan sat, panting with mixed emotions, one of them being gratitude that Michael did save his life. He sat there, weak to the bone, his back to the street below, holding on for dear life to his precariously tilted wheelchair on the roof floor in front of him.

When he finally caught his breath, he looked at Michael, who was still on his knees with a gash on the right side of his fore-head generously flowing blood down his cheek and on to the roof floor. "Michael, I knew you didn't want to kill me. But my god, why all the drama?"

Michael sat there, a bloody mess; he looked at Ivan and smiled. He was grateful to see him still alive.

CHAPTER 13
THE PAYOFF

"It is not in the stars to hold our destiny, but in ourselves."—
William Shakespeare

Michael got up off his knees and sat on the roof floor staring up at Ivan. He removed a handkerchief from his pocket and compressed the wound on his forehead to stop the bleeding. "No Ivan, I had no intention of killing you, far from it. But I did want to know about my father, and I did want to know if you truly had killed him."

"I did, I admit it. But he had it coming to him. As I said *it was just business, Michael, just business.* And besides, he wasn't the father for you. Look at the life you created for yourself! Trust me, you did much better without him."

"Trust you? You know, Ivan, your sense of logic and morality amazes me. You do just as you damn well please, whatever fits best for you in your world, and if it violates common decency and the law, you have the perfect explanation as to why the law and morality don't apply to you. How in the world did you ever come to this way of living?"

Ivan stared and thought for a moment. "Look Michael, if you grew up as I did in a housing project in one of the most violent sections of Moscow, one that makes the South Bronx look like Beverley Hills, you would have the answer to your question. Life can't always fit into your neat boxes of American morality and legalities. Sometimes you gotta' take what you can, while you can, no matter what! Otherwise, you're not long for this world."

"Really, Ivan? I can understand your challenging beginnings. But a world like you paint is one of chaos, unbridled crime and eventually total destruction."

Ivan, looking down at his wheelchair, had moved to a level of contemplation, the kind you do when thinking about your past. "Michael, you just have no idea. My parents were Jews. My father was a low-level banker who worked for the state. When he got caught arranging our family's escape from the Soviet Union to Israel, he was immediately sentenced to 20 years in Siberia. I never saw him again. He probably died there."

"And my mother, she was a saint and a real beauty. One of the KGB agents, who raided our apartment and took my father away, had eyes for her and would often visit our flat. I think the real reason for imprisoning my father was so he could get close to my mother. I can't tell you how many times I came home unexpectedly and heard that horrible commotion in her locked bedroom. Crying in terror, she would beg him not to touch her, but it was useless. Once, when I tried to get in to help her, that big bastard came out and punched me mercilessly across the room. I was in the hospital for a week."

"I guess she couldn't stand it anymore. A few months later, when I came home I found the police and the coroner at our apartment complex. She had jumped to her death from our apartment on the 10th floor."

"After that there was nothing left for me in Moscow. I hooked up with a neighborhood gang until I raised enough cash to buy my escape to Europe and then the U.S."

"So, Michael, don't tell me about your values and how life should be. Unless you've been where I have, you have no idea."

"Ivan, you're right. We have little in common, and I could never understand what you had to endure in your life. But you maliciously killed my father, and I can't let that go. I can forgive you, but you have a debt to society that you must pay."

"I got what I came for. I know more about my father, and yes, it isn't very pretty. But, Ivan, you can't get away with having killed him."

"Whaddaya mean? I did get away with killing him, and he deserved it! Now, Michael, please help me off this damn ledge and back onto my chair. Let's get the hell out of here and go for a peacemaking drink. Whaddaya say?"

Nearly recovered from his fall, Michael stood up, staggered a distance slowly up the slanted roof, turned around and looked at Ivan, who was still sitting on the retaining wall with his back to the street 65 floors below. He pulled a small black metal device from his coat pocket and held it in the air. "Ivan, do you know what this is?"

"No, I have no idea. A telephone?"

"No, Ivan. It's one of those amazing advances in Silicon Valley technologies and it's my close 'friend.'"

"Michael, what the hell are you talking about? Get me off this ledge, damn it!" "Wherever I go, my 'friend' always goes with me. It sits comfortably in my jacket pocket. I could be on a train, a plane, in my car, running in the park, or just walking in the forest. If I have an idea I want to remember for later, I simply have to say it out loud, not very loud, and this device records it. What's neat about it is that it is voice activated and can be programmed to a specific voice to turn it on. Once, it's on, it stays on for a set period—I usually set it for 10 minutes—and it stays on as long as it continues to hear my voice within that 10-minute period. Another useful advanced function is its noise cancellation circuitry. It only records human voices, and it has a small, but powerful micro-speaker."

Ivan was still lost. After all that had happened, he had no idea as to what Michael was talking about. With that, Michael pushed a button and it began to play the entire discourse between the two of them while on the roof, from the moment Ivan became conscious.

"You see Ivan, it has two settings, a short-range personal recording setting, which is what I use all of the time, and a longer range conference setting. I had never used that function before, but it seems to work quite well, don't you think?"

Ivan's expression changed to the cold monster he truly was. "And just what do you expect to do with that, Michael?"

"On the ride here from Brooklyn, I was thinking about what to do with you. I concluded that you have to pay for killing my father. As you say, '*It's just business, Ivan, just business.*' You're going to spend the rest of your miserable life in a prison cell. How long that will be in your condition, I have no idea. But you have to pay for what you did to my father."

"Michael, you must be kidding. We've become friends over these past weeks. You almost lost your life while saving mine a short time ago. You can't be serious."

"I'm very serious. I can forgive you, but I could never justify and condone your wholesale murder of my father, no matter what he did to you. When we get down to the lobby, I will arrange for the police to take you and my little 'friend' here into custody; then I'm finished with you Ivan, for good."

"Michael, please! I... I can make it worth your while."

"Sorry, Ivan; I'm a reasonably forgiving guy, but my soul hasn't yet reached that level of enlightenment. You have to pay for what you've done. Call it karma."

Ivan and Michael looked at each other. Not a word was said for the next several minutes.

Ivan was at first very frightened, but then slowly, very slowly, a pale look of resignation came over him. His gruff voice was now barely audible. "Michael, I'm not going to rot in some miserable prison cell with this disease. It just ain't gonna happen." "I'm sorry, Ivan that's just the way it's going to be."

Then, in a fading whimper, his voice cracking, "Not really, Michael." And with that, Ivan Prostor pushed towards the ledge with all of the strength he had left in him, jettisoning himself off the ledge, wheelchair and all, into the space of his final destiny.

Michael ran down the roof from where he had been standing and jumped as quickly as he could to catch some part of Ivan.

He shouted in desperation, "Nooooo, Ivan, nooooo!" But this time he was too far away to be of help.

Ivan screamed and he screamed and he screamed for what seemed like an eternity to Michael, but was only about seven seconds until his 200-plus pound body came face- to-face in a single instant with the street below. Then all was quiet. Both he and his wheelchair hit the gutter with the full force of Newton's gravitational field. Fortunately, there was no collateral damage to anyone or anything. A crowd gathered quickly to view the grotesque splatter of both man and machine.

Michael didn't look over the edge. He didn't have to, he knew what was there. He stood in a suspended animation of shock. This was not what he had planned. Ironically, he felt a not insignificant sense of loss and guilt. Should he have done things differently? At times, the universe can take a strange and cruel path. But, it's never one to question, just one to learn from. It's always karma. That's the way the universe works.

Michael had learned a lot in the past several weeks. He would never be the same. He was deeply sorry for Ivan's death and yet, he had a more complete sense of being, who he really was, where he came from, and perhaps even a glimpse of where he was going. This chapter of his life was over.

CHAPTER 14
CLOSURE

"It's because the door hasn't been closed yet that the nightmares still find their way in."—**Joyce Rachelle**

The next day, in the late afternoon, Michael was sitting in his living room in meditative reverie staring out the large door to his patio. It had been an unseasonably warm day so the door was open as the sun was beginning to set. He still felt pain for what had happened to Ivan, yet paradoxically also a deep sense of relief as he sipped a cool glass of iced tea. No more wine for a while.

Then it happened. Michael's reverie was broken in an instant. Just as before, he saw a screaming, falling man pass by the view in his window. But this time, it was clearly a different person than the first two events he experienced. The man, dressed in a dark suit and a bright pink shirt, appeared to be having intense convulsions, his arms and legs in contorted spasms. As he passed by Michael's field of view, a wheelchair followed immediately thereafter in his path. Michael didn't move or react.

He stoically reached for another sip of iced tea. He didn't get up to inspect the street scene. He knew what was there, or rather, not there. He also knew in the deepest part of his soul that this was the last of the *Fallen* he would ever see from the building across the way. Ivan's contorted philosophical business ethic came to mind, *"It was just business, Michael just business."*

Minutes later, his cell phone rang and broke his detached contemplation. It was Sophia. "Michael, Michael, did you see today's New York Times?

"No, Sophia, should I?"

"Michael, listen to this. 'Ivan Prostor, one-time gangster, thug and racketeer yesterday jumped to his death in what police say was caused by his depression over a neurological disease he had been fighting for the last few years.' Police can't understand how he got up the stairs to the roof with his wheelchair. But, it appears they're not concerned. His death has been ruled a suicide; case closed! And Michael, guess where he chose to end it all?"

"Where, Sophia?"

"The building across from your condo, the one from which I just know he pushed your father to his death!"

"Interesting, Sophia, I guess what goes around, comes around."

"Michael, you don't seem moved at all by this turn of events!"

"I am very much moved, Sophia...Believe me, very much so."

Michael was quiet for more than several moments.

Sophia gasped, "Michael...Michael...Did...did you have anything to do with this?"

She waited for his response..."Good night, Sophia; sleep well. I love you."

After a long pause, Sophia managed a whisper, "Good night, Michael; I love you too."

About the Author

James A. Cusumano (www.JamesCusumano.Com) is chairman and owner of Chateau Mcely (www.chateaumcely.cz/en/homepage), chosen in 2007 by the European Union as the only "Green" 5-star, castle hotel in Central Europe, and in 2008 by the World Travel Awards as *The World's Leading Green Hotel*. Chateau Mcely offers programs that promote the principles of Inspired and Conscious Leadership, finding your Life Purpose and Long-Term Fulfillment.

He began his career during the 1950s in the field of entertainment as a recording artist. Years later, after a PhD in physical chemistry, business studies at Stanford University and as a Foreign Fellow of Churchill College at Cambridge University, he joined Exxon as a research scientist and later became their research director for Catalytic Science & Technology.

Dr. Cusumano subsequently cofounded two public companies in Silicon Valley, Catalytica Energy Systems, Inc.—devoted to clean power generation; and Catalytica Pharmaceuticals, Inc., which manufactured drugs via environmentally-benign, low-cost, catalytic technologies. While he was chairman and CEO, Catalytica Pharmaceuticals grew in less than 5 years, from several employees to 2,000 and became more than a $1 billion enterprise.

Subsequent to his work in Silicon Valley and before buying and renovating Chateau Mcely with his wife Inez, Dr. Cusumano returned to entertainment and founded Chateau Wally Films (www.chateauwallyfilms.biz), which produced the feature film

What Matters Most (2001: www.imdb.com/title/tt0266041), distributed in more than 50 countries.

He is the coauthor of **_Freedom from Mid-East Oil_** (2007) and author of **_Cosmic Consciousness – A Journey to Well-being, Happiness and Success_** (2011), **_BALANCE: The Business—Life Connection_** (2013) and **_Life Is Beautiful: 12 Universal Rules._**

Dr. Cusumano lives in Prague with his wife Inez and their daughter Julia.

A Thought from the Author

We live in progressively complicated and challenging times, and yet paradoxically, there is an ever increasing level of consciousness. I assert this, despite all of the misgivings and unfortunate happenings across our planet. There are growing numbers of men, women and even children, who are deeply touched by these events and are working diligently "behind the scenes" to make this a better and sustainable humanity.

The purpose of this series of novellas is to create deeper thinking about currently unexplainable phenomena in the world of consciousness, those that appear to have no logical basis and therefore are generally rejected as nonsense and nonexistent. Paranormal concepts such as remote viewing, the *Akasha Field* and telepathy are just a few examples.

Deeper thinking requires that we move beyond our current level of consciousness to a higher plane, one that can provide answers you would not observe in the tussle of your day-to-day experiences. It's all wrapped up in consciousness, more precisely ***Cosmic Consciousness***, which I have explored in great detail elsewhere.[1,2]

Beyond my daily practice of meditation and other means to mindfulness, I found a simple exercise that can have positive

---

1 James A. Cusumano, *Cosmic Consciousness: A Journey to Well-being, Happiness and Success*, Fortuna Libri, Prague, 2011.
2 James A. Cusumano, *Life Is Beautiful: 12 Beautiful Rule*, Waterside Productions, Cardiff, CA 2016.

effects and increase mindfulness. I call it *My Notes, My Life*. In the following pages, I share it with you for your personal consideration.

Each page presents a characteristic trait or emotion that we may experience from time to time. Under each label is a quote to stimulate your reverie on the subject, as well as a space to write your thoughts. Allow me to share a personal example for an emotion all of us feel at various times throughout our life.

> **ANGER** *("You will not be punished for your anger; you will be punished by your anger"* —Buddha):*"Today, I was writing a letter to a dear friend, and my ten-year-old Julia was driving me crazy, interrupting me with what I thought at the time were trivial questions. I yelled at her to go to her room and play there. A few moments later, I felt the pain of my action. I knew her questions were not trivial, and were more important at the time than my letter writing. I went into Julia's room and asked if I could play with her. She stood up from where she was playing with her toys and held my hand. We smiled at each other."*

When the spirit moves you, perhaps you may want to address one small thing that touched you that day. Consider jotting down just a sentence or two as to why it was special or enlightening. Occasionally, look at your notes. You may be surprised at how they recall a moment that made you feel closer to **Cosmic Consciousness**. It can be a healing experience to both your body and soul.

My Notes, My Life!

HOPE

"Hope is being able to see that there is light despite all of the darkness."

Desmond Tutu

COMPASSION

"Compassion is the keen awareness of the interdependence of all things."

Thomas Merton

ANGER

"You will not be punished for your anger; you will be punished by your anger"

Buddha

Consciousness

FORGIVENESS

"Forgiveness is the final form of love."

Rheinhold Niebuhr

LOVE

"To Love someone deeply gives you strength; being loved by someone deeply gives you courage."

Lao Tzu

FAITH

"Faith is an oasis in the heart which will never be reached by the caravan of thinking."

Khalil Gibran

MINDFULNESS

"We need to practice mindfulness if we want to have a future, if we want to save ourselves and the planet."

Thich Nhat Hanh

HAPPINESS

"True happiness is to enjoy the present without anxious dependence upon the future."

Lucius Annaeus Seneca

REGRET

"Never look back unless you are planning to go that way."
Henry David Thoreau

SELF PITY

"Self pity is easily the most destructive of the non-pharmaceutical narcotics; it is addictive, gives momentary pleasure and separates the victim from reality"

John Gardner

LONELINESS

"The most terrible poverty is loneliness, and the feeling of being unloved."

Mother Teresa

PASSION

"Passion is one great force that unleashes creativity because if you're passionate about something, then you're more willing to take risks."

Yo-Yo Ma

COMMITMENT

"Commitment is what translates a promise into a reality."
Abraham Lincoln

ENVY

"Envy comes from people's ignorance of, or lack of belief in, their own gifts."

Jean Vanier

NOW

"True power is within, and it is available now."

Eckhart Tolle

INTEGRITY

"Integrity is doing the right thing, even when no one is watching."
C. S. Lewis

TRUTH

"Truth is like the sun. You can shut it out for a time, but it ain't goin' away."

Elvis Presley

WISDOM

"Knowledge speaks, but wisdom listens."

Jimi Hendrix

CREATIVITY

"The worst enemy to creativity is self-doubt."

Sylvia Plath

GRATITUDE

"Gratitude unlocks the fullness of life. It turns what we have into enough, and more. It turns denial into acceptance, chaos into order, and confusion into clarity. It can turn a meal into a feast, a house into a home, a stranger into a friend."

Melody Beattie

www.ingramcontent.com/pod-product-compliance
Lightning Source LLC
Chambersburg PA
CBHW071334130626
46556CB00004B/1899